This book belongs to:

This Book started at:
Little Free Library #45480
Elburn, IL #LiteraryLands

LITTLE FREE LIBRARY.org ™
TAKE A BOOK • RETURN A BOOK

The stories in this collection were previously published individually by
Candlewick Press, 2067 Massachusetts Avenue, Cambridge, MA 02140

First published by Walker Books Ltd.
87 Vauxhall Walk, London SE11 5HJ

Based on the Audio Visual series "Maisy." A King Rollo Films production for
Universal Pictures International Visual Programming. Original scripts by Andrew Brenner and Jeanne Willis.
Illustrated in the style of Lucy Cousins by King Rollo Films Ltd.

First edition in this form 2005
ISBN: 0-7607-9604-1

This edition published specially for Barnes & Noble, 2005 by Candlewick Press

2 4 6 8 10 9 7 5 3 1

Printed in China

This book was typeset in Lucy Cousins.
The illustrations were done in gouache.

Candlewick Press
2067 Massachusetts Avenue
Cambridge, Massachusetts 02140

visit us at www.candlewick.com

At Home with Maisy

Maisy

Lucy Cousins

CANDLEWICK PRESS

CAMBRIDGE, MASSACHUSETTS

Maisy Makes Gingerbread

Maisy is in her kitchen today.

She is going to make gingerbread cookies.

Maisy needs flour, sugar, butter, eggs, and ginger.

Maisy mixes everything together.

She rolls out the dough and cuts out different shapes.

Maisy puts the cookies into the oven.

Maisy licks the bowl while the cookies are baking.

Then she washes up.
Ding, Dong!
That's the doorbell!
Who can it be?

It's Charley and Tallulah!

Just in time for an afternoon snack.

Yum, Yum.
Nice gingerbread
cookies, Maisy.

Doctor Maisy

Hello, Doctor Maisy.
Hello, Nurse Tallulah.
Let's play hospital!

Tallulah listens to Maisy's heartbeat. That tickles!

Panda is sick today. Maisy listens to his heartbeat. Thump, thump, thump!

Maisy takes Panda's temperature.

Oh, no.
Panda has a *fever*.

Panda needs to rest. Maisy carries him up the stairs.

Night-night, Panda.
Get well soon.

Tallulah calls
from downstairs.
Maisy! Maisy!

Maisy runs
down the stairs.

Careful,
not too fast!

Crash!
Maisy bumps into Tallulah.

Ouch!

Tallulah wraps
Maisy's nose
in a bandage.

That's better!
Bye-bye, Nurse Tallulah.
Bye-bye, Doctor Maisy.

Maisy Takes a Bath

It's Maisy's bathtime.

She runs the water and puts in some bubbles...

and in goes Duck.

Ding, Dong!
Oh, that's
the doorbell.

Maisy runs
downstairs to
see who it is.

Hello, Tallulah.

Maisy can't play now. It's her bathtime.

Maisy runs back upstairs and gets undressed.

Maisy jumps into the bubbly bath.

Ding, Dong!
Who is ringing the doorbell now?

Hello again, Tallulah!
Maisy is still taking her bath. Come and play later.

Oh! Where are you going, Tallulah?

Tallulah runs up
to the bathroom
and takes off
her clothes.

Splash, splash!

Maisy and Tallulah play in the bath.

Hooray!

Maisy's Bedtime

Maisy is sleepy.
It's time for bed.
It's bedtime for
Panda, too.

Maisy closes her bedroom curtains.

Tuwhoo, tuwhoo, hoots the owl.

Maisy washes her face and brushes her teeth.

Maisy puts on her pajamas.

Maisy gets into bed and reads a story.

But where is Panda?

Is he in the
toy box?

Oh, there he is!

Maisy turns off the light.

But she still isn't ready to go to sleep.

Maisy forgot to use the toilet!

Panda sits on his potty, too.

Maisy is very sleepy now.

Good night, Maisy.
Good night, Panda.